Little Transfer Book

Unicorns

with over 600 transfers

Illustrated by Camilla Garofano
Designed by Emily Beevers
Edited by Hannah Watson & Felicity Brooks

Turn to the last page to find
out how to use the transfers on
the right-hand pages of this book.
Use pens or crayons to decorate
the left-hand pages.

Opal

Topaz

Moonstone

Holly

Cinnamon

Luna

Astrid

Nova

Peppermint

Frost

Sparkle

Crystal

Snowdrop

Juniper

Misty

Marina

Mistletoe

Aspen

Ivy

How to use the transfers

You'll need a pencil or ballpoint pen to add the transfers to the right-hand pages and fill the scenes with unicorns. First, take the transfer sheets out of their pocket at the front of the book and find the one with the symbol that matches the symbol on the page you want to work on. (Most sheets contain the transfers for two scenes.) Carefully remove the backing sheet.

To use the transfers, position one of the little pictures over the place you want it to go in the scene.

Scribble all over it firmly on the front of the sheet with a pencil or ballpoint pen. Take care not to touch the pictures around it.

When you have completely covered the transfer, gently lift off the transfer sheet to reveal the new picture.

First published in 2018 by Usborne Publishing Ltd., Usborne House, 83-85 Saffron Hill, London, EC1N 8RT, England. Printed in China.